W9-AZU-257

It Takes Two

By Lesile Budnick
Illustrated by The Thompson Brothers
Based on the characters by Ron Rodecker

Published by Creative Edge, LLC, 2006, an imprint of Dalmatian Press, LLC, Franklin, Tennessee 37067.
No part of this book may be reproduced or copied in any form without written permission from the copyright owner.

Visit Dragon Tales on the Web at www.dragontales.com
Printed in China
ISBN: 1-40378-042-0

06 07 08 09 ZHE 10 9 8 7 6 5 4 3 2 1
CE10159 Dragon Tales 8x8 HC Storybook: It Takes Two

Emmy was painting quietly when Max wandered into the playroom. Max liked to paint too, so he grabbed a paintbrush. "Purple, please," he said.

"Max, isn't there something else you'd rather do?" grumbled Emmy. "We don't *always* have to play together."

"Then I'm going to Dragon Land!" announced Max, taking out their magical dragon scale.

Emmy dropped her brush. "Me too!" she cried, reaching for the scale. Together they chanted:

"I wish, I wish with all my heart
to fly with dragons in a land apart."

Max and Emmy arrived at the School in the Sky, where it was Dragon Parent Day. Everyone was busy preparing for the party and the show—everyone except Zak and Wheezie.

"I want to decorate dragonberry cupcakes," said Zak.

"I want to hang streamers," said Wheezie.

"Sisters!" muttered Zak.
"Brothers!" grumbled Wheezie.
"I know what you mean," said Emmy.

"I wish we didn't have to do everything together!" complained Zak and Wheezie.

At that, a glowing green gnome appeared. Smiling, he said:

"Come one or two, here's an offer for you.
Say a wish in rhyme and I'll make it true!"

Zak and Wheezie looked at each other and nodded. Zak closed his eyes and said:

"Dragons are purple, dragons are green. . . ."

Wheezie blurted out:

"I wish we were two, with room in between!"

Poof! With Zak and Wheezie's wish, one two-headed dragon became two one-headed dragons. Zak stared at Wheezie. Wheezie stared at Zak.

"Your wish has been granted," said Quetzal. "Now you don't have to do everything together. You can do as you like."

"I'm going to hang streamers everywhere!"
Wheezie said joyfully.

"And I'm going to decorate the best
dragonberry cupcakes ever!" said Zak.

And off they went in separate directions.

Wheezie jumped into the air and did a wild loop-the-loop. She swooped down, grabbed the streamers, and crisscrossed through the room, swirling and twirling, back and forth, again and again. "Loooove it!"

Finally the whole room was filled with color. Wheezie was thrilled with her creation. She couldn't wait to show her brother. "Zaky, where are you?"

But Zak didn't hear Wheezie. He was too busy decorating dragonberry cupcakes in the next room. First, he neatly frosted them. Then he carefully chose the decorations—sparkling fairy sprinkles for his father, colored doodle-dots for his mother, and one with munchy musical notes for his sister. "Perfect," he said. "I can't wait to show Wheezie." He looked up from his work. "Where is she?"

Zak and Wheezie came looking for each other. "Wow, those cupcakes look *deee*-licious!" said Wheezie. "Now come see what I've done all by myself, Zaky."

Zak loved Wheezie's streamers. "Super-duper job, Sis!"

Then he remembered something. "What about the show?" said Zak. "How can we perform together if we're apart?"

"You'll just have to practice doing it as two," suggested Emmy.
"I guess it couldn't be too hard," said Zak.
"C'mon! Let's give it a try," said Wheezie.

So Zak and Wheezie tried. But with four arms, four legs, four wings, two tails, and so many scales, they kept getting tangled.

"I don't want to be apart *forever*!" cried Zak.

"It was fun decorating cupcakes on my own, but I miss the way we used to do other things together."

"Me too!" said Wheezie.

"*Niños*," Quetzal said kindly, "nobody is keeping you apart. You can be together again whenever you wish."

"So we can make another wish?" Zak asked.

"Of course!" Quetzal replied. Then he clapped three times.

Clap! Clap! Clap! The tiny green gnome magically reappeared.

Zak and Wheezie looked at each other and smiled.
"Being apart was once our dream," said Zak.
"It was good to be two . . . " said Wheezie.
Then they finished together, "But we'd rather be—*a team!*"

Poof! Zak and Wheezie were back together again just as the school bell rang. It was time for the show!

Soon it was Zak and Wheezie's turn.

"May I present," Quetzal announced, "Zak and Wheezie!"

The duo sang:

> "Together again, so happy are we,
>   even if sometimes we just don't agree."

They finished their song and took a bow. Everyone cheered.
Max and Emmy cheered the loudest.

"When we get home, if it's okay with you, I'd like to paint together," said Max.

Emmy thought for a minute.

"Definitely," she said. "It wouldn't be the same without you!"

Wheezie smiled at Zak. "Brothers! I just looove them!" she sang.
Zak hugged his sister.

"Bravo!" said Quetzal. "And *muchas gracias* to all my students for making this the best Dragon Parent Day ever!"